KU-760-054

PETER the PUMPKIN-EATER

4

PETER

the

PUMPKIN-
EATER

For Rob, who filled our garden
with elephant-sized pumpkins

Chapter One

Young Peter the Pumpkin-Eater's involvement with plants started when he entered the "Grow and Show" competition, held every year at the Garden Society Headquarters.

Peter wasn't the gardening type. He was only interested in winning first prize – a mountain bike – for the most unusual plant.

However, there was a slight hitch to Peter's competition début. He didn't have a green thumb or a green finger or, for that matter, any other green part of his body.

Flower beds, vegetable patches, parks, and jungles were all very foreign to city-slicker Peter. The only jungles that he was aware of were concrete ones.

Peter would have loved to cultivate a carnivorous plant. Insect-snapping Venus flytraps are always a big hit. However, Peter finally decided to grow cactuses because he liked the sound of some of the names: jumping cholla, prickly pear, and organ pipe.

But, more important, he wanted to grow cactuses because he'd heard that just about anyone could do it.

9

Twice a day, Peter lovingly fed compost and water to his cactuses. He talked to them in his most caring and soothing voice and played calming piano music for them.

But, sadly, in just over one week, Peter saw the mountain bike slipping out of his reach. His cactuses weren't doing well.

11

Chapter Two

For three days and three nights, Peter moped around, wishing he hadn't gone overboard with the compost and water.

But, finally, he snapped out of it when he saw a poster advertising a concert at the zoo. Peter had a great idea, and he couldn't wait to put his plan into action.

13

14

A couple of days later, while everyone else was busy watching the giraffes sway and the band play, Peter walked to the back of one of the enclosures to ask the zookeeper for something that would save his wilting cactuses.

15

And the zookeeper knew just the thing – elephant manure! She gave Peter permission to shovel as much of the cactus-reviving stuff into his wheelbarrow as he could haul away.

After Peter politely thanked the zookeeper, he raced home to feed his cactuses the new secret remedy. For obvious reasons, as he chatted away to them, Peter purposely neglected to mention exactly what it was that he was giving them.

Chapter Three

No one, not even the zookeeper, could have predicted what was going to happen over the next few months. Peter's backyard turned into a jungle. Untamed, elephant-sized pumpkin plants stampeded over Peter's cactuses.

How was Peter to have known that the zookeeper had fed pumpkins to the elephants?

But all was not lost. Peter, being an optimist, decided that the prize for the largest and heaviest vegetable – a new pair of rollerblades – was just as good as a mountain bike.

By the time the day of the competition arrived, Peter was the proud owner of not one, but a "herd" of ninety-eight elephant-sized pumpkins.

Peter selected the largest and heaviest pumpkin, placed it on a go-kart, then hauled it off to the Garden Society Headquarters.

The vegetable section was very easy to find. The overgrown turnips, leeks, marrows, and other vegetable varieties made it look like a giant's garden.

Judging the giant vegetable competition were Mrs Daisy Chain, from the daisy division of the Garden Society, and Mrs Rosie Bush, representing the rose division. Despite having soft spots for daisies and roses, respectively, both of the judges could still get excited over such things as Peter's elephant-sized pumpkin. After all, as Mrs Daisy Chain said, "Every plant is part of nature's wonder."

After much weighing and measuring, oohing and aahing, the two judges awarded Peter's pumpkin first prize. Mrs Daisy Chain firmly planted a first-prize rosette on the pumpkin, and Mrs Rosie Bush gently placed the rollerblades on Peter's feet. It was a proud moment for Peter and his family, a family that, for many generations, had managed to create only dust bowls for gardens.

Chapter Four

The first thing Peter did when he got home was to try to tame the "herd". Elephant-sized vines and leaves had to be chopped back. He set up a stall, aptly named "The Pumpkin Patch", and put his prized produce up for sale.

When the other gardeners heard about the sale, they rushed over to Peter's stall to purchase the award-winning pumpkins. Obviously, they were after the elephant-sized seeds for next year's competition.

That left seventy-six pumpkins. Luckily, just as Peter was starting to feel desperate, he got a call from the local children's theatre. The theatre was going to put on a production of *Cinderella* and needed a pumpkin for the coach.

That afternoon, the actors playing the two mean sisters, the wicked stepmother, and the coachman hauled off a huge pumpkin. They couldn't wait to show the props department their lucky find.

Peter then had to get rid of only seventy-five pumpkins. But thanks to a newsletter to the members of the rose division of the Garden Society, of which Mrs Rosie Bush was the editor-in-chief, Peter was swamped with requests to buy his elephant-sized pumpkins. Everyone wanted jumbo-sized jack-o'-lanterns for Hallowe'en, which, thankfully for Peter, was in just three days.

40

Peter decided that the only way to get rid of the remaining pumpkins, once and for all, was to eat them. So he set out to make all the pumpkin dishes that he could find recipes for: pumpkin soups, pumpkin muffins, pumpkin pies, pumpkin pancakes, pumpkin soufflés, and loads of pumpkin chips.

Because none of his family liked pumpkin, Peter had to live up to his nickname Peter the Pumpkin-Eater, which was given to him around this time.

Finally, Peter restored the backyard to its former dust-bowl glory. He decided to keep his beloved cactuses, as they fitted in very well with the desert look that his parents found so easy to maintain.

At next year's competition, Peter hopes to win the mountain bike with his most unusual cactus. Meanwhile, he still sings and chats away to his precious prickly pals, but he is *very* careful about what he feeds them.

From the Author

The idea for this story came to me a little while after my family and I decided to give our plants elephant manure. But imagine our surprise when we discovered what the elephants had been eating!

After we chopped back the vines, we tried to find ways to get rid of the pumpkins. Like Peter, we made a lot of pumpkin dishes. But, unlike Peter, we didn't get a visit from two mean sisters and a wicked stepmother!

We have now moved away from the house where we grew elephant-sized pumpkins. In our new house, our "garden" is a window box. Cactuses and succulents thrive in it. They are easy to look after, and I can chat and sing away to them all year round.

When I sing the nursery rhyme *Peter, Peter Pumpkin-Eater* to my daughter, Rosie, it always makes me giggle to think of the fun that my family and I had trying to tame our very own "herd of elephants" in our backyard!

Janine Scott

From the Illustrator

I have been illustrating books for the past ten years. My best drawings are those in which I have illustrated something I know about, so I also like to base characters on people I know.

Unlike Peter's family in *Peter the Pumpkin-Eater*, my family – especially my mum – can grow just about anything, and with amazing results. Once, she grew a crop of gigantic pumpkins, just like Peter's, for my sons.

My dad chose the biggest pumpkin and carefully cut a jack-o'-lantern face in it. The pumpkin was too big to be lit up by a candle, so when it became dark, we went outside and put an electric lamp inside it. The enormous jack-o'-lantern sat, glowing and grinning, on our front lawn.

Sandra Cammell

Peter the Pumpkin-Eater

ISBN 13: 978-0-79-011665-5
ISBN 10: 0-79-011665-0

 Kingscourt

Published by:
McGraw-Hill Education
Shoppenhangers Road, Maidenhead, Berkshire, England, SL6 2QL
Telephone: 44 (0) 1628 502730
Fax: 44 (0) 1628 635895
Website: www.kingscourt.co.uk
Website: www.mcgraw-hill.co.uk

Written by **Janine Scott**
Illustrated by **Sandra Cammell**
Edited by **Frances Bacon**
Designed by **Nicola Evans**

Original Edition © 1997 Shortland Publications
English Reprint Edition © 2009 McGraw Hill Publishing Company

All rights reserved.

Printed in China through Colorcraft Ltd., Hong Kong